To my favorite
Ninja neighbors,
Nika and Alik
— CRS

To David,
my own stealthy ninja
— RG

For Jodi
— DS

G. P. PUTNAM'S SONS
an imprint of Penguin Random House LLC
375 Hudson Street, New York, NY 10014

Library of Congress Cataloging-in-Publication Data is available upon request.

Manufactured in China.
ISBN 978-0-399-17626-5
1 3 5 7 9 10 8 6 4 2

Design by Ryan Thomann. Text set in Markin.
The art was done with Sumi brush work on rice paper
and completed in Adobe Photoshop.

BEWARE

HENSEL AND GRETEL NINJA CHICKS

Corey Rosen Schwartz and Rebecca J. Gomez

illustrated by Dan Santat

G. P. PUTNAM'S SONS

Once upon a menacing time
two chicks knew a fox was at large.
Their Ma had been taken
and Pop was quite shaken
so Hensel and Gretel took charge.

They trained in the art of **ninjutsu**
and practiced their wing throws and blocks.

They learned how to creep
without making a peep
so they wouldn't fall prey to that fox.

One day they returned from the dojo
to a coop in complete disarray.
The signs of a tussle
showed someone with muscle
had dragged
their dear papa
away!

They quickly surveyed their surroundings.
The fox had left prints in the dirt!
"Come on, we're not chicken!
That fox needs a lickin'
before our poor papa gets hurt!"

They trekked till
they spotted a feather.

It looks like
we're on
the right track!

They kept up the chase,
dropping crumbs, just in case,
so they'd easily find their way back.

The forest grew twisted and tangled
as Hensel and Gretel searched on.
The light faded fast
and they noticed at last
that the trail—
and the breadcrumbs—
were GONE!

They shuddered and groped in the darkness. "We're lost!" whispered Hensel with dread.

They weaved and they wound,
and kept roaming around
until they saw light up ahead.

"I'll whip up some quick teriyaki,
while we wait for the tea cakes to bake."
"Why not?" Hensel reckoned,
off-guard for a second.

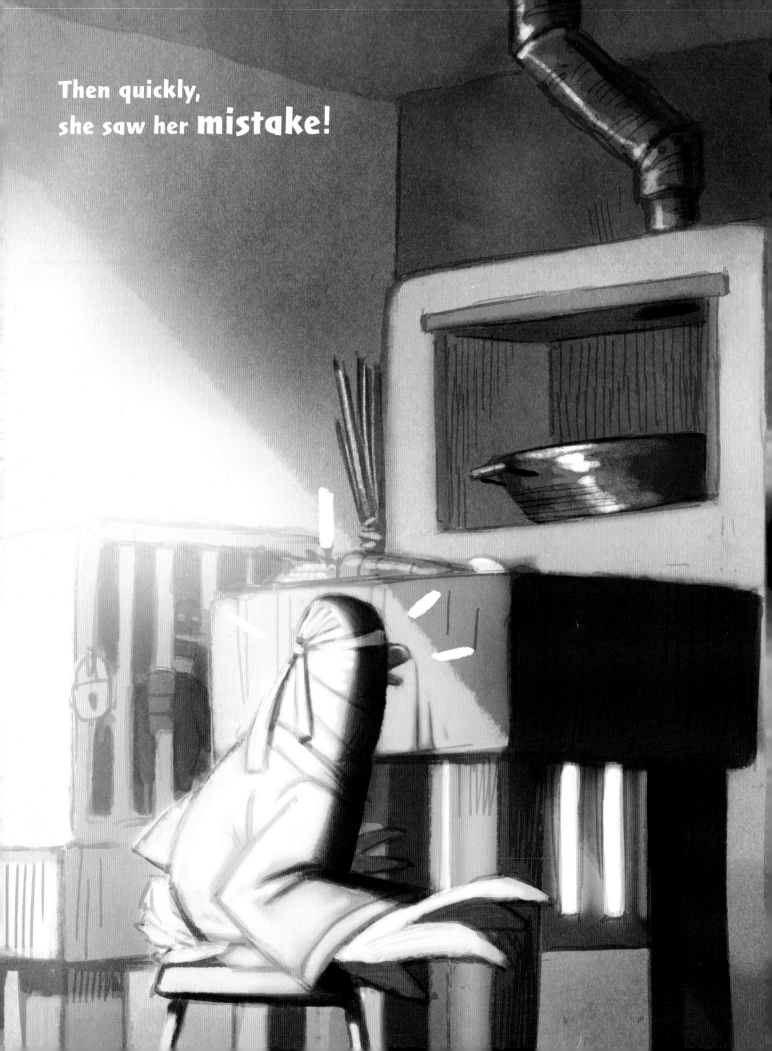

She gasped, and then dashed
    to the corner,
where Pop was confined in a crate.
"**Watch out!**" Papa cried.

"*You'll be*
chicken-pot-pied!"

She sidestepped,
but it was too late.

The fox plucked her up in a hurry
and shoved her right into the pen.

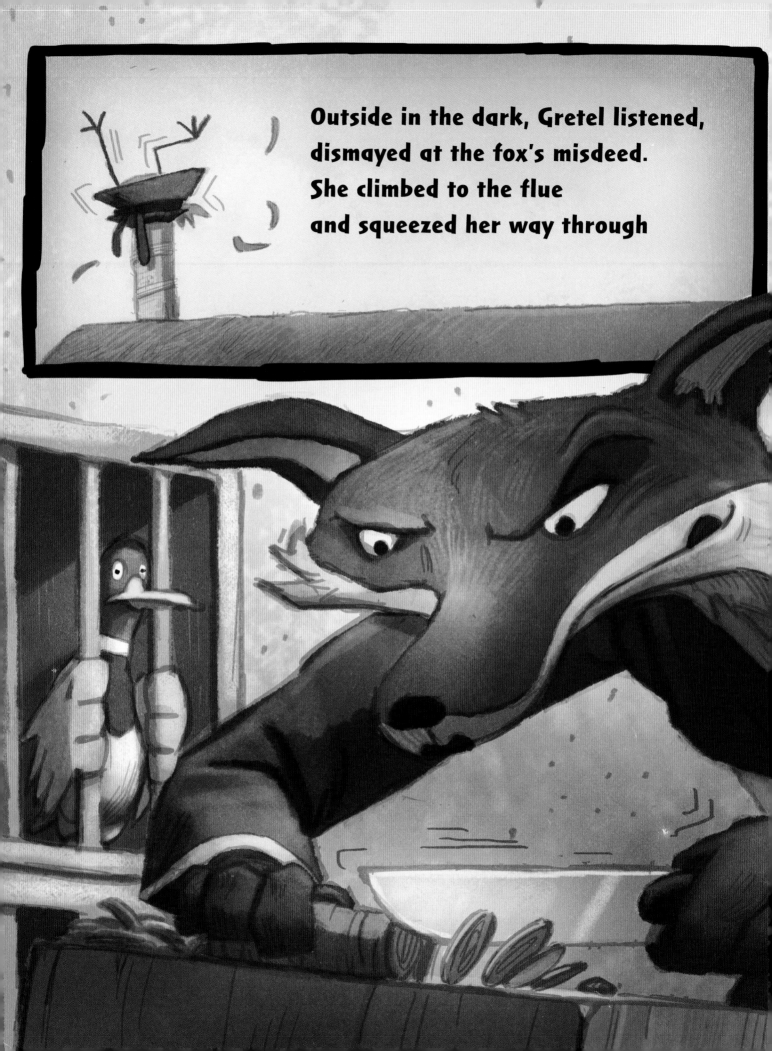

Outside in the dark, Gretel listened,
dismayed at the fox's misdeed.
She climbed to the flue
and squeezed her way through

Then Gretel swooped in
and snatched Mama
and swiftly adjusted her stance.

The fox took a **leap**,

"Not bad," said the fox, striding toward them.
"Give up!" Gretel clucked, undeterred.

The fox said, "Surrender?
No way, **chicken tender!**
Your cheep little threats are absurd!"

The fox charged and grappled with Gretel—
a flurry of feathers and fur.

The fox held her tight,
but Gretel wrenched right

as something zipped past with a whir!

With the fox in a daze, Gretel vaulted as Hensel and Papa broke free.

She slammed the door shut
and then locked it.

The fox crumpled, looking unnerved.

"You two Ninja Chicks
got us out of that fix,
and **justice** — not dinner — was served."

From then on they made it their mission
to **rescue**, **protect** and defend.
They'd work night and day
to liberate prey
till bird-napping came to an end.